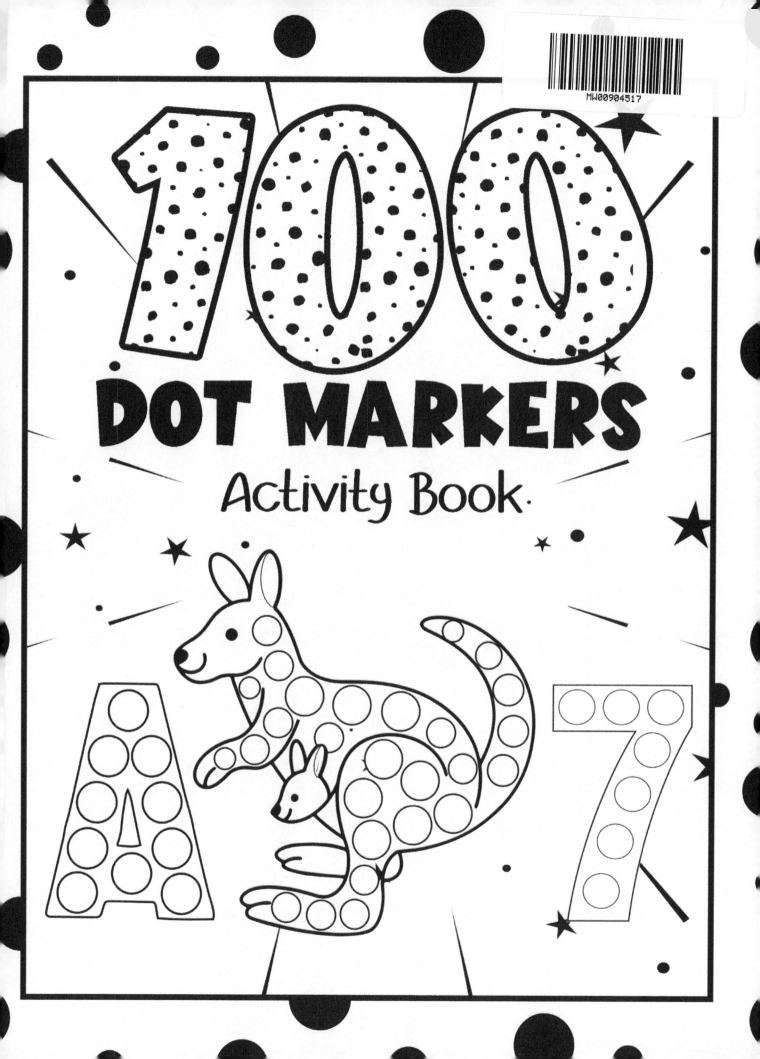

100 DOT MARKERS
Activity Book.

CHAPTER 1
LETTERS

A

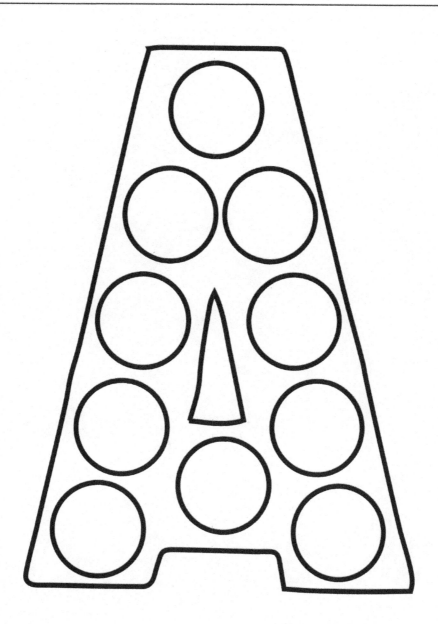

A

B

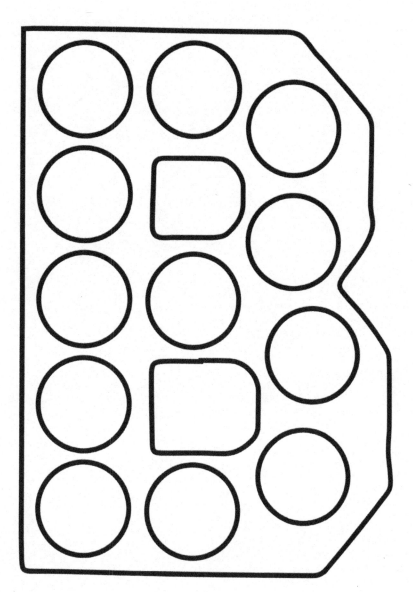

B

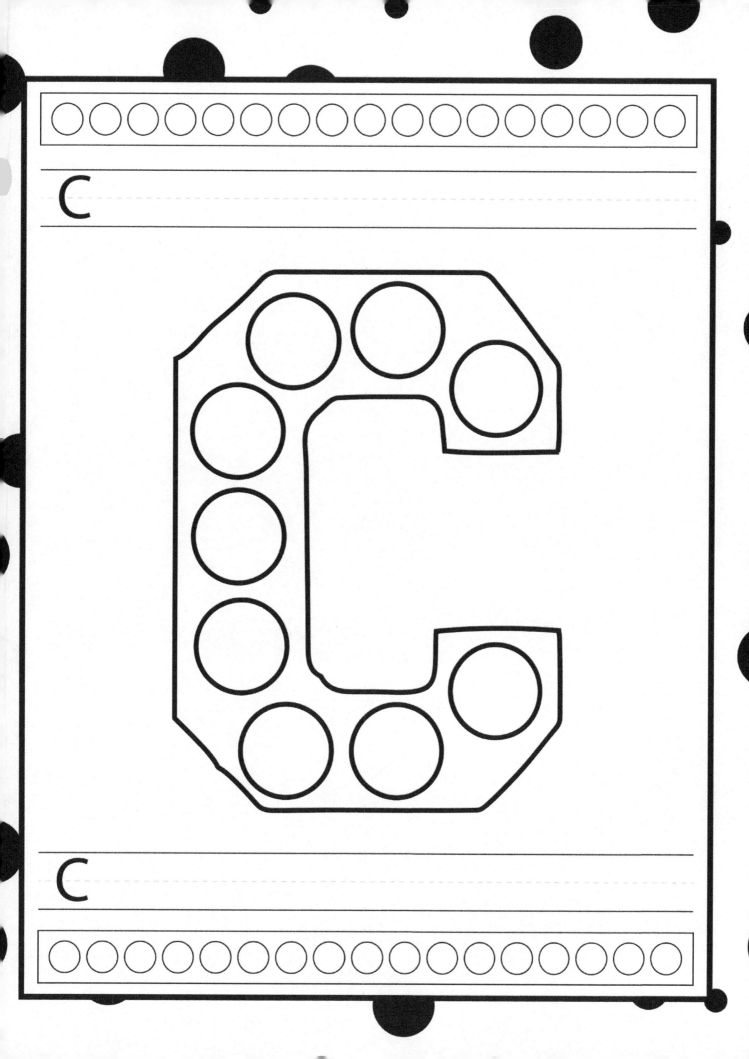

D

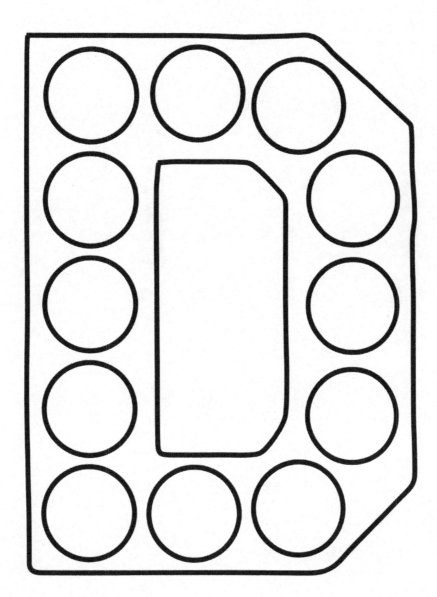

D

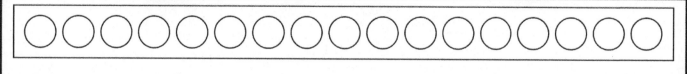

E

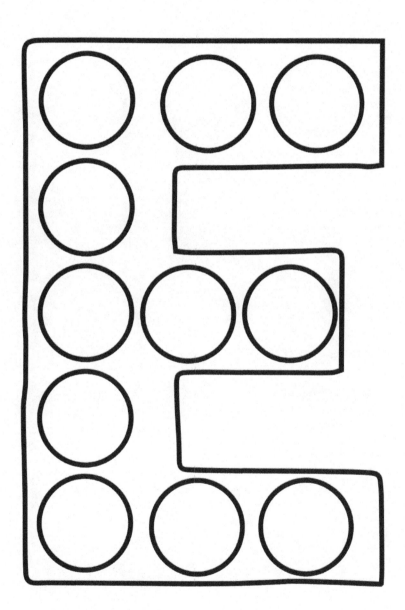

E

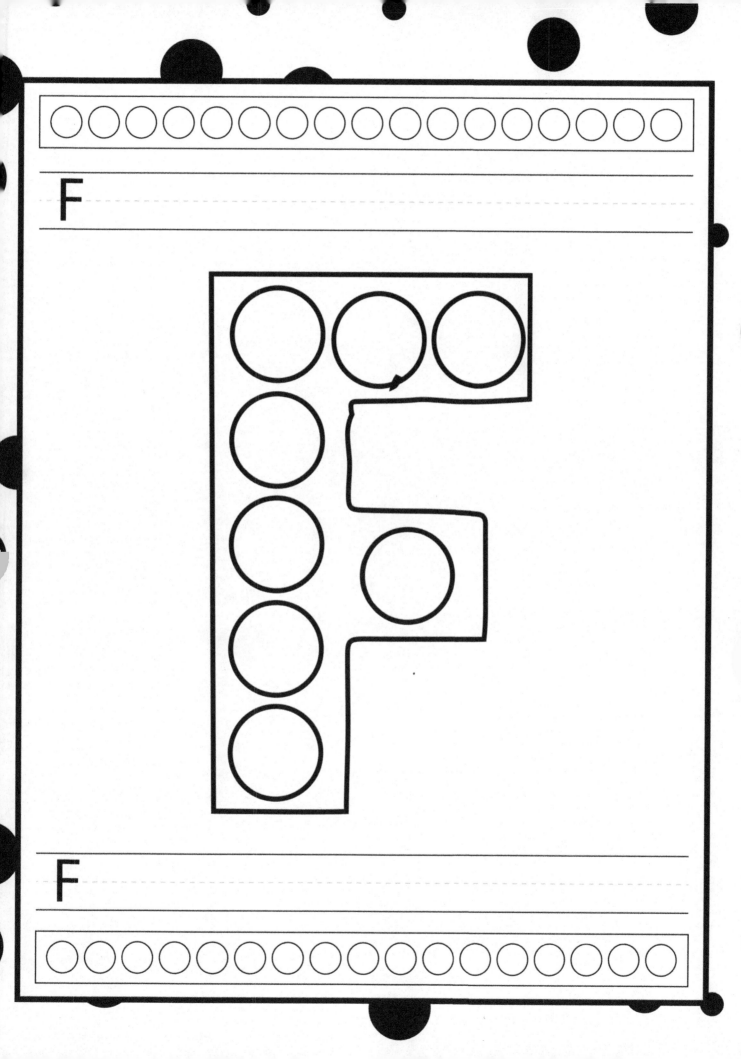

F

F

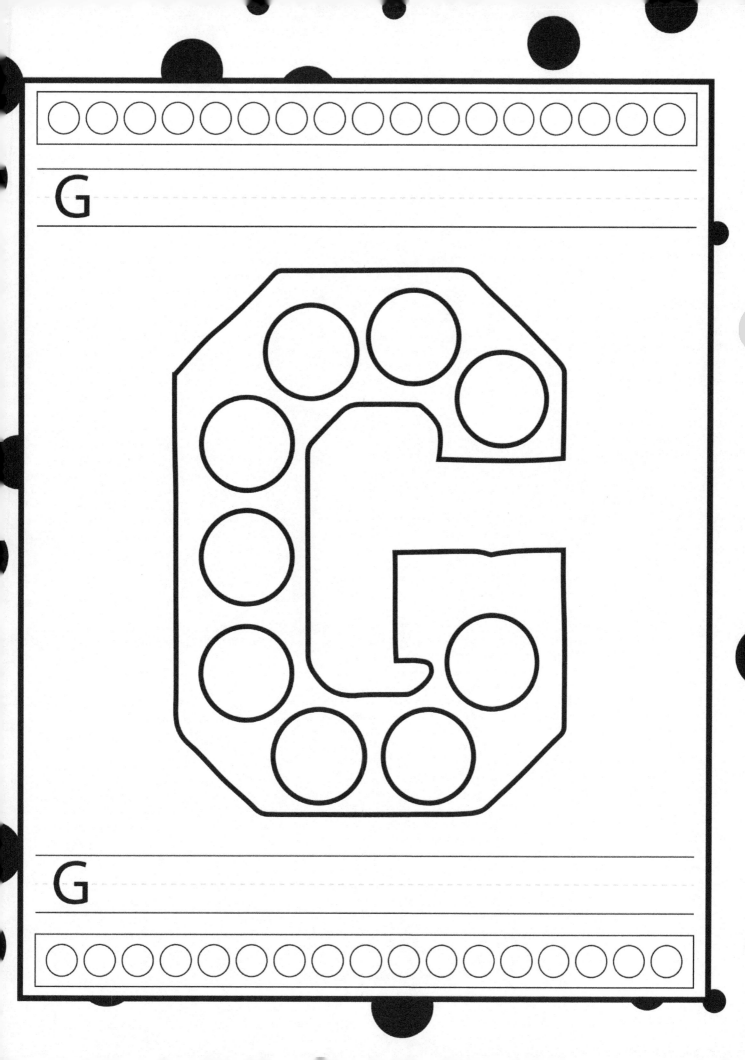

G

G

H

H

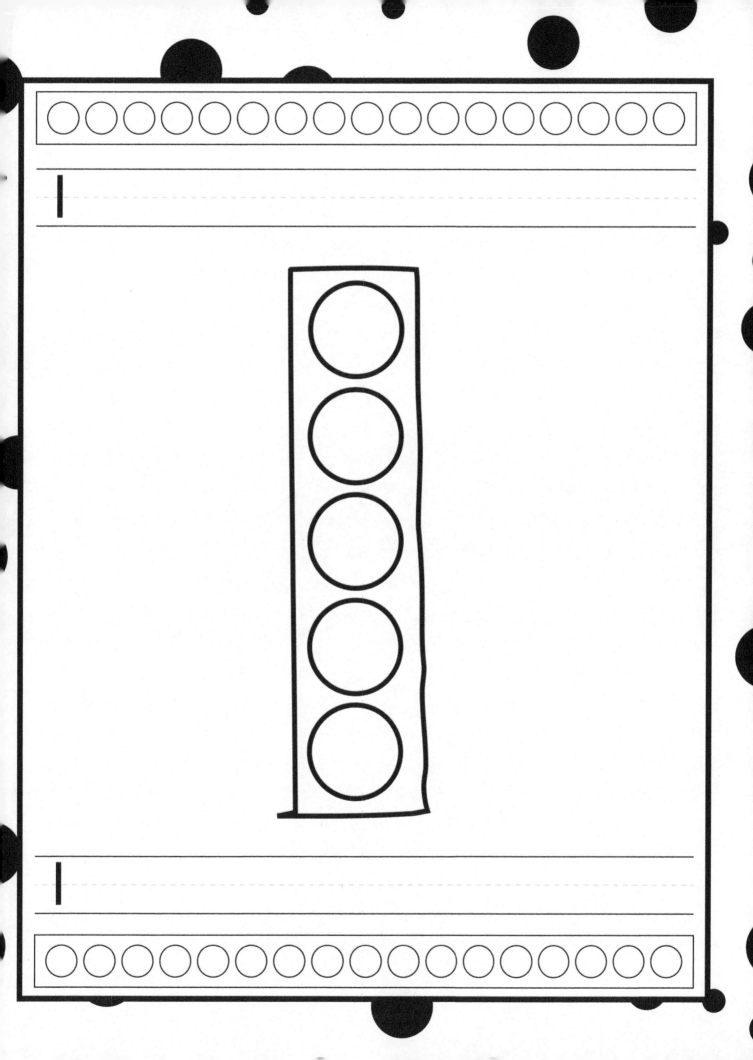

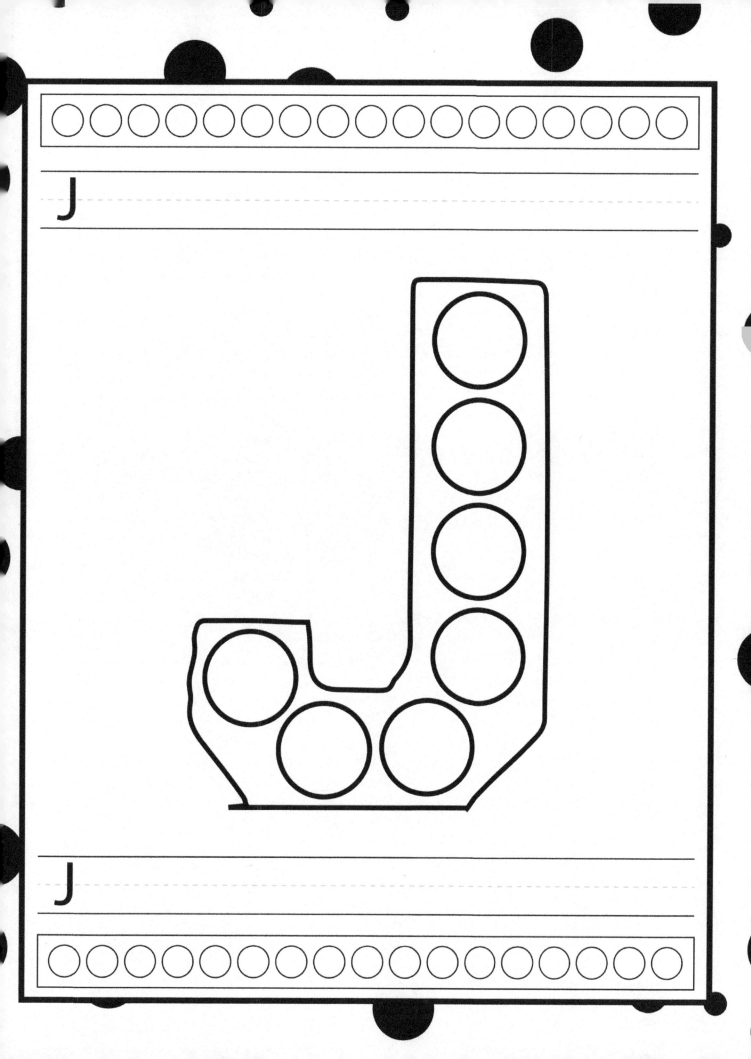

K

K

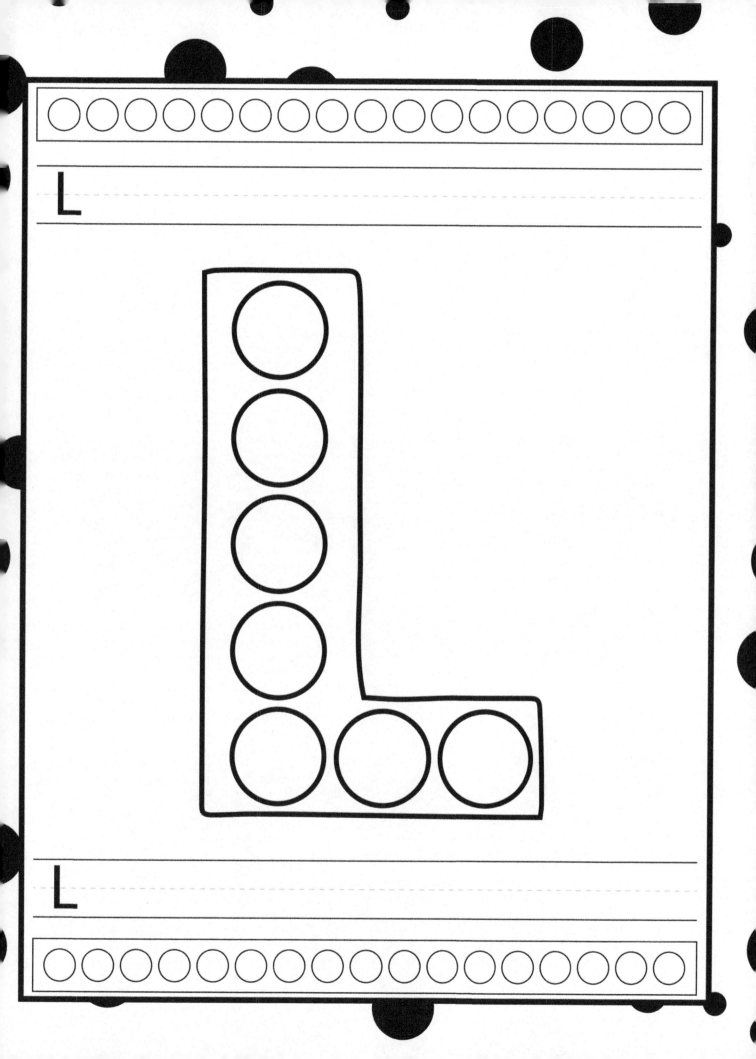

M

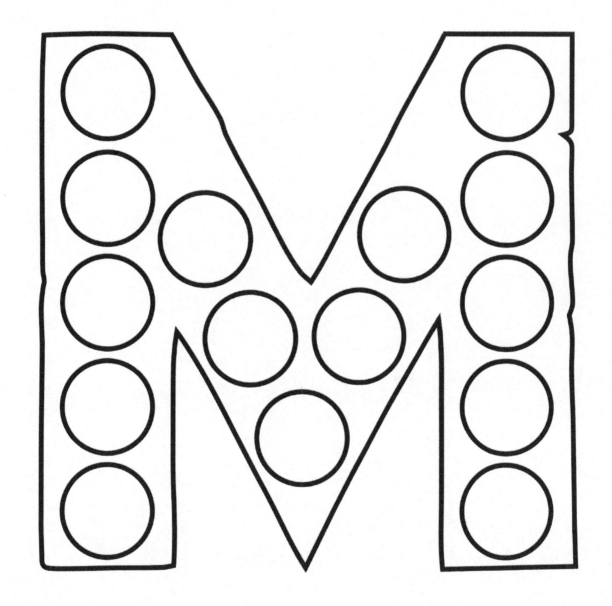

M

N

N

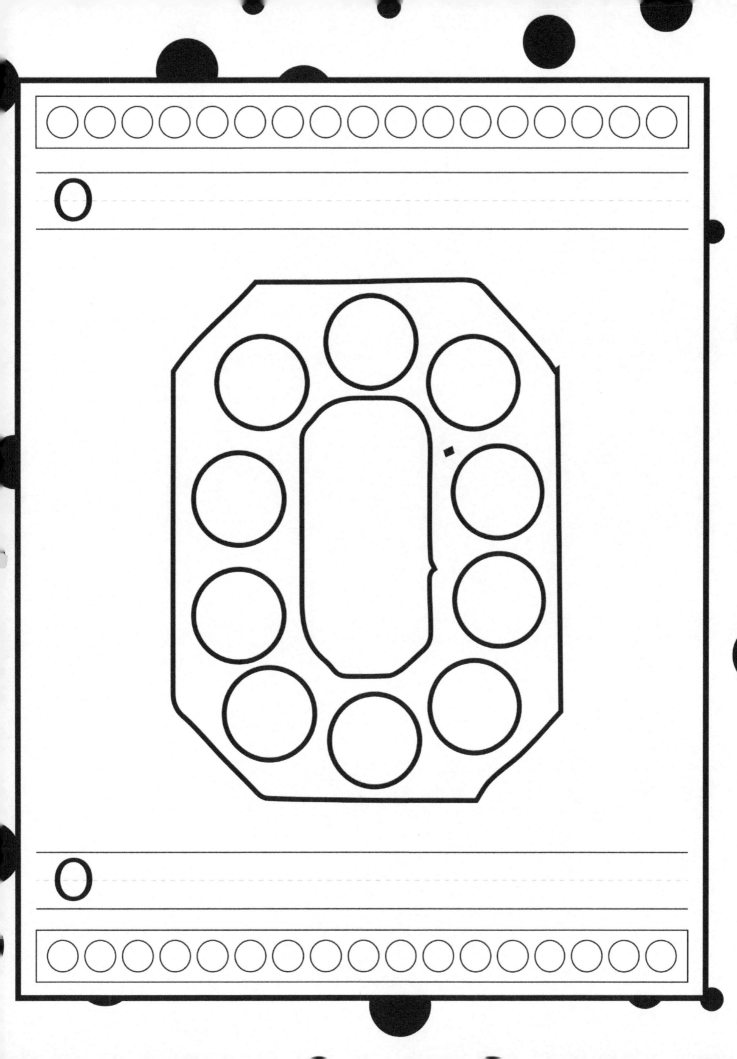

P

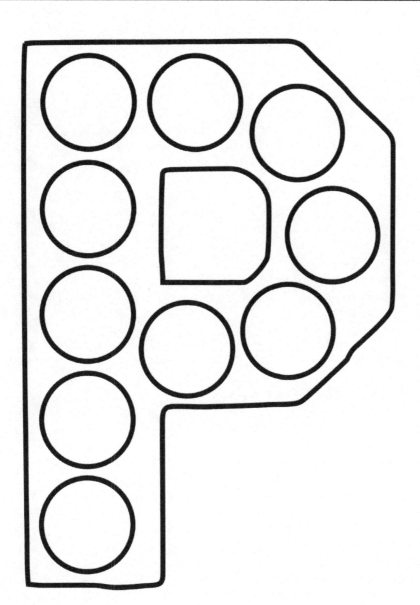

P

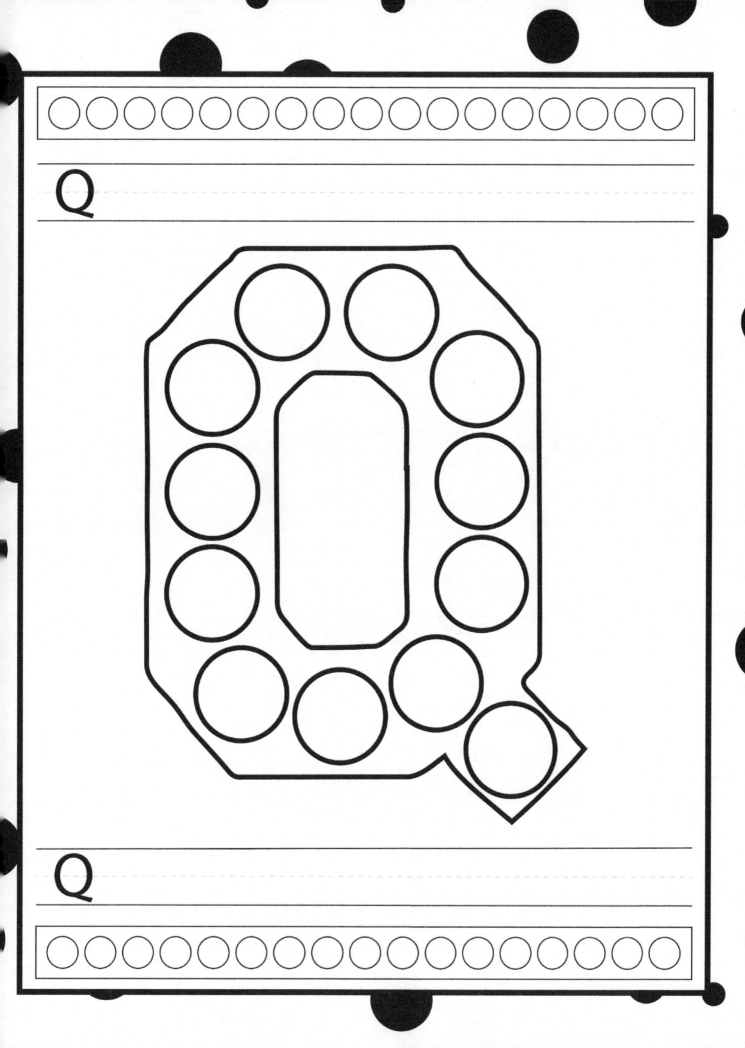

Q

Q

R

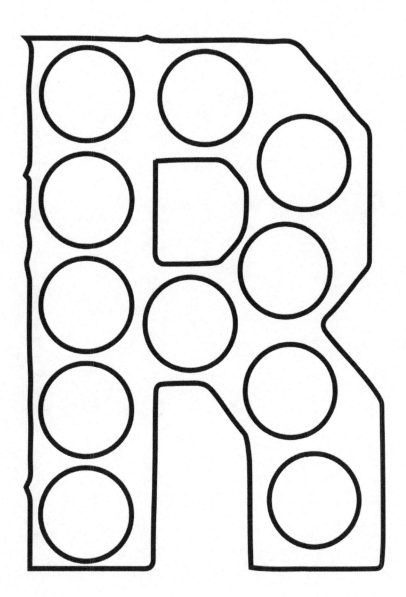

R

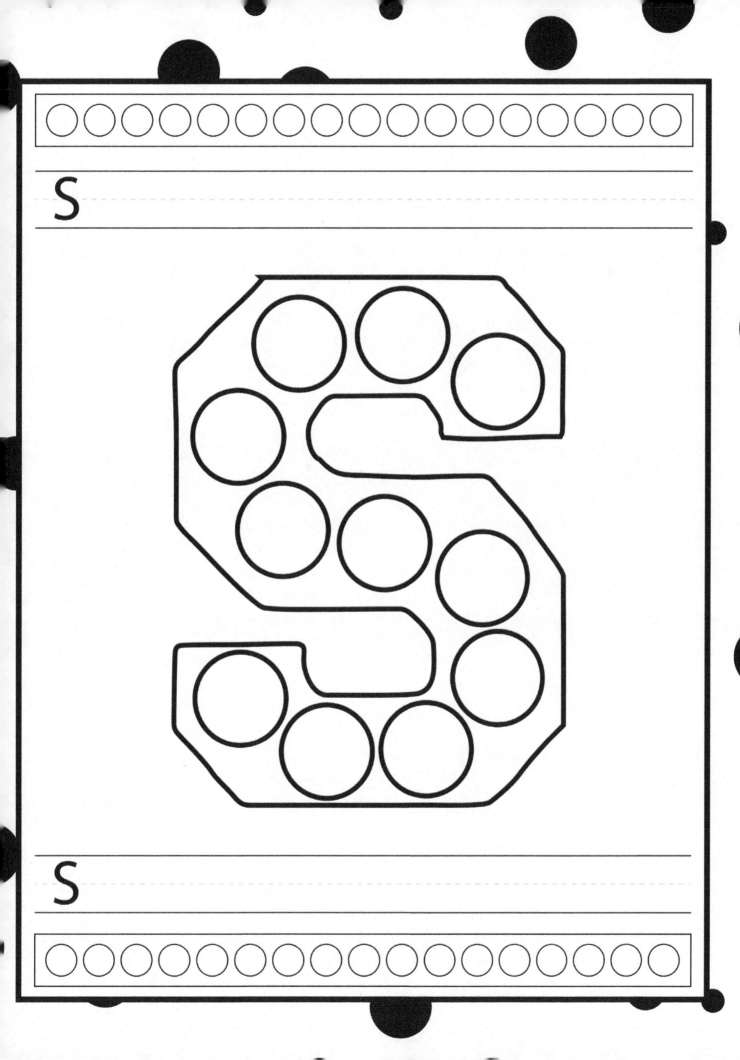

S

S

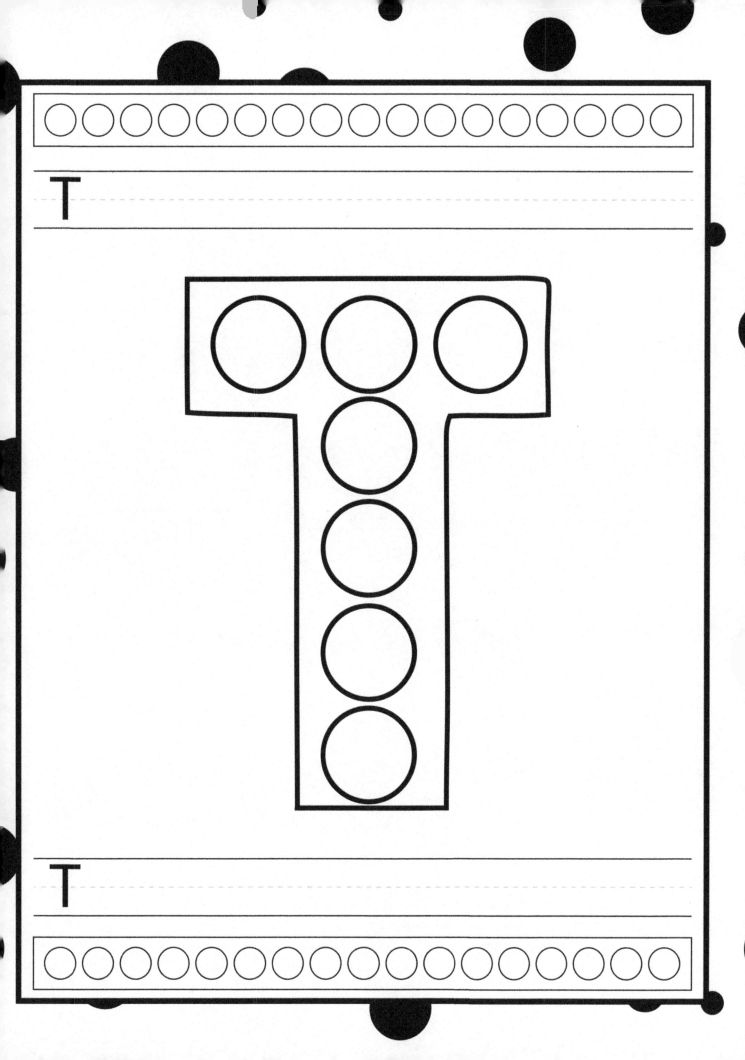

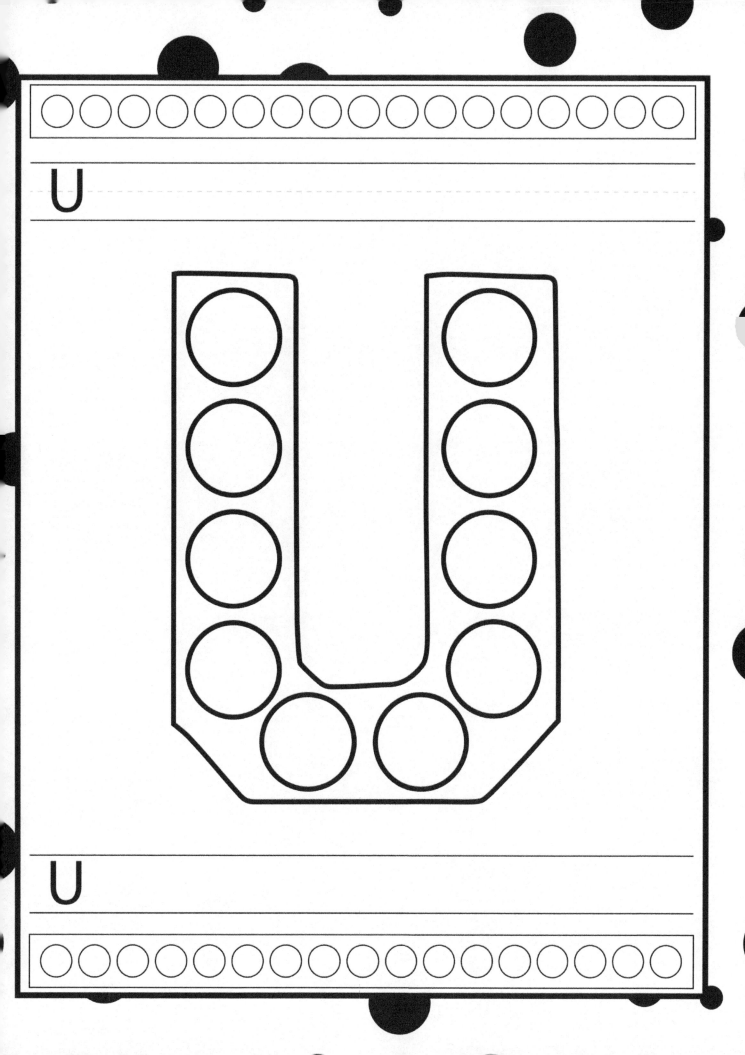

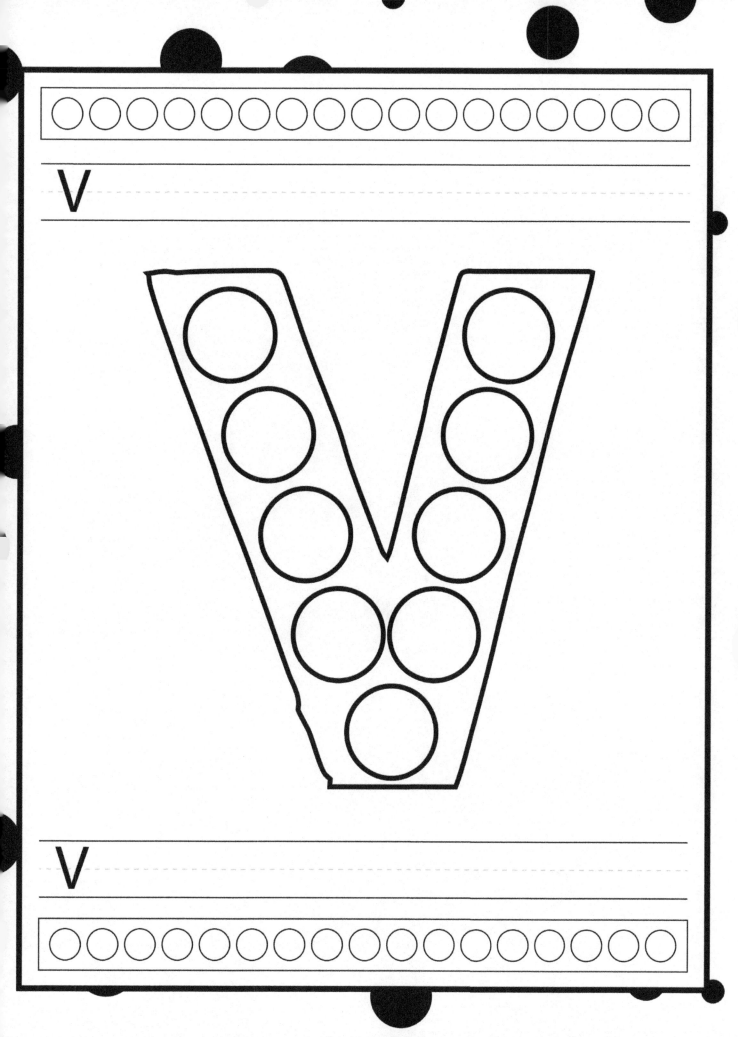

W

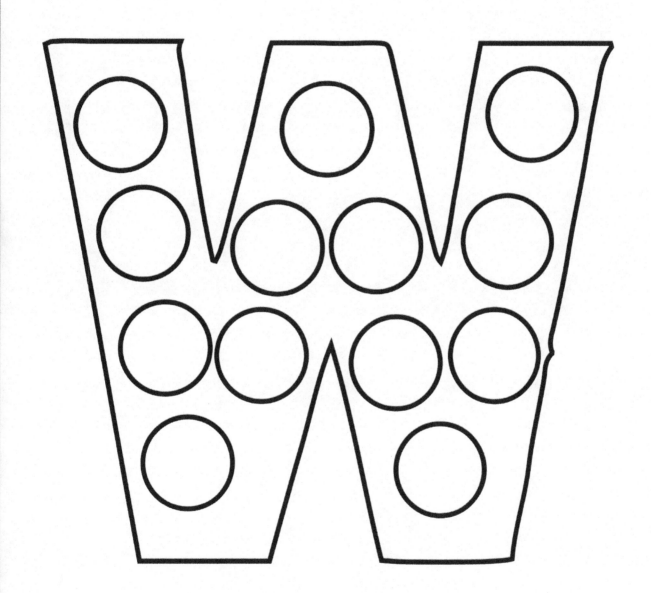

W

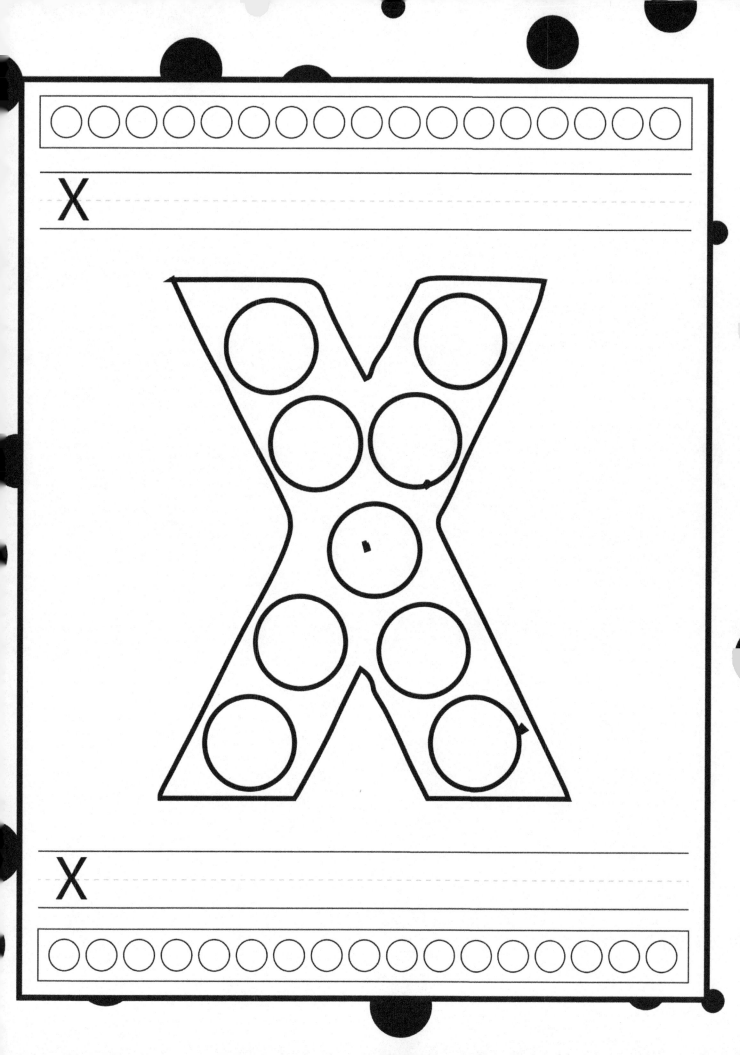

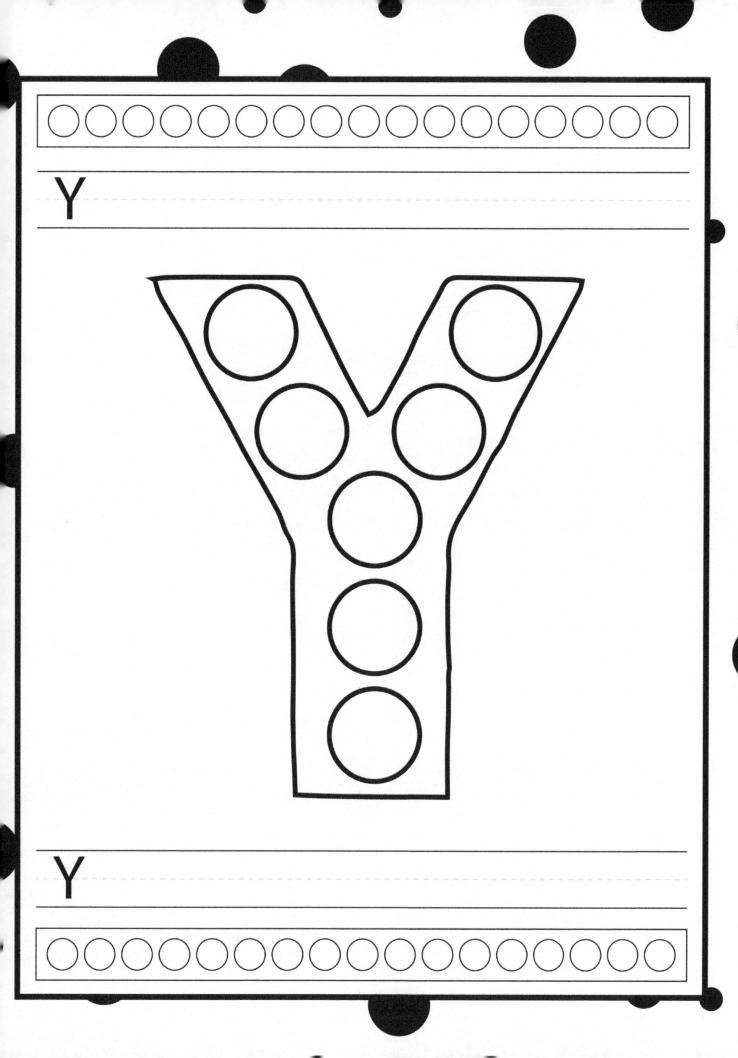

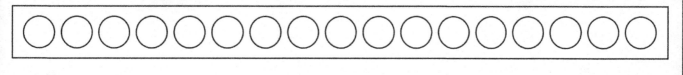

Z

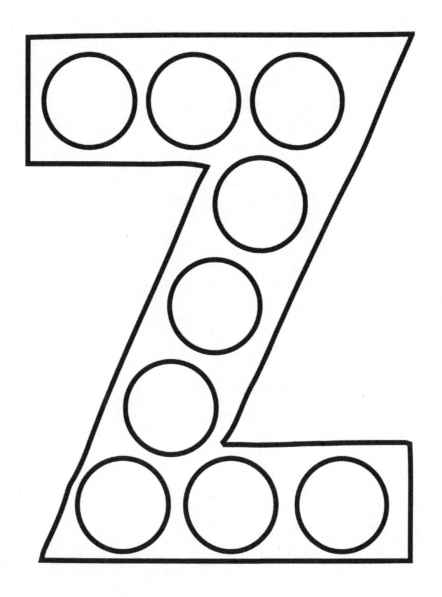

Z

CHAPTER 2
NUMBERS

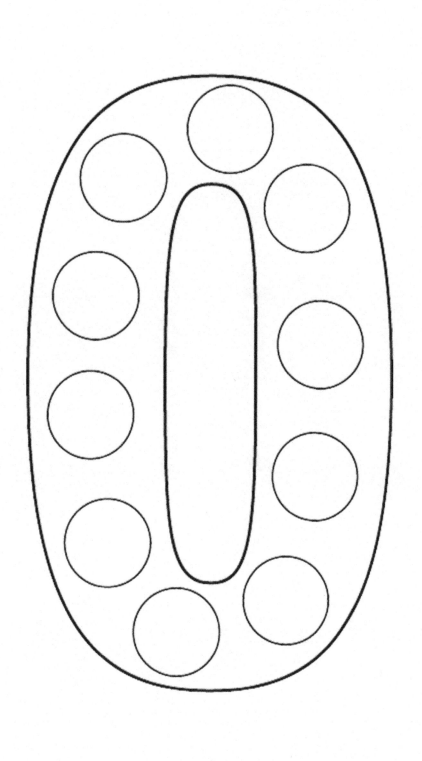

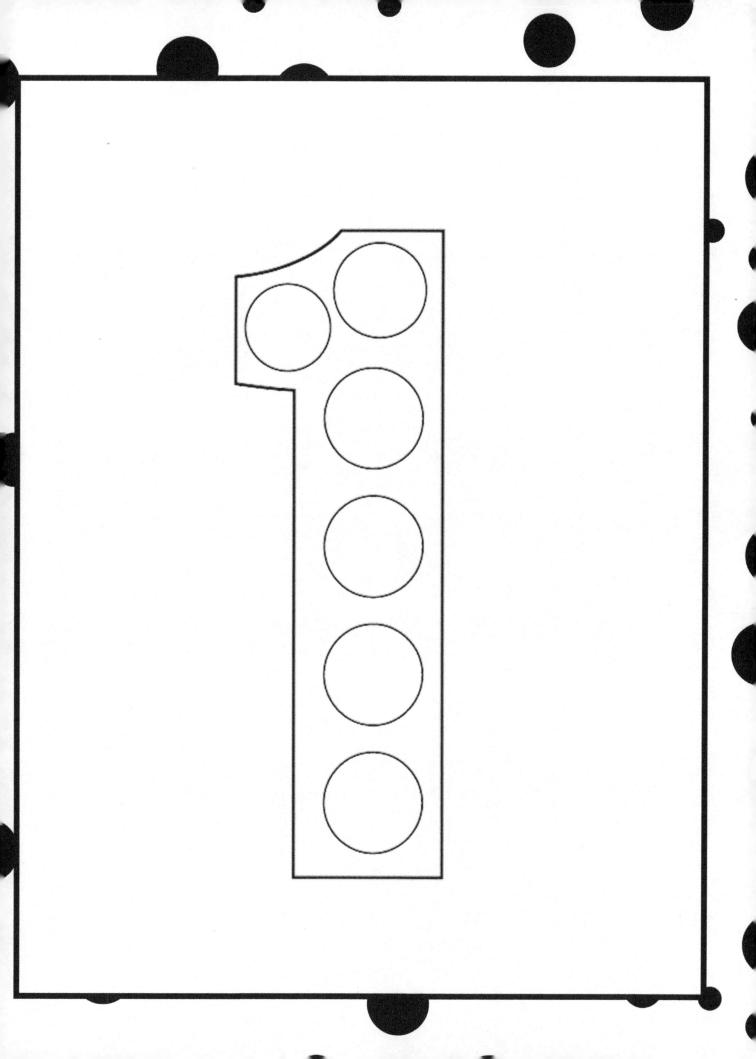

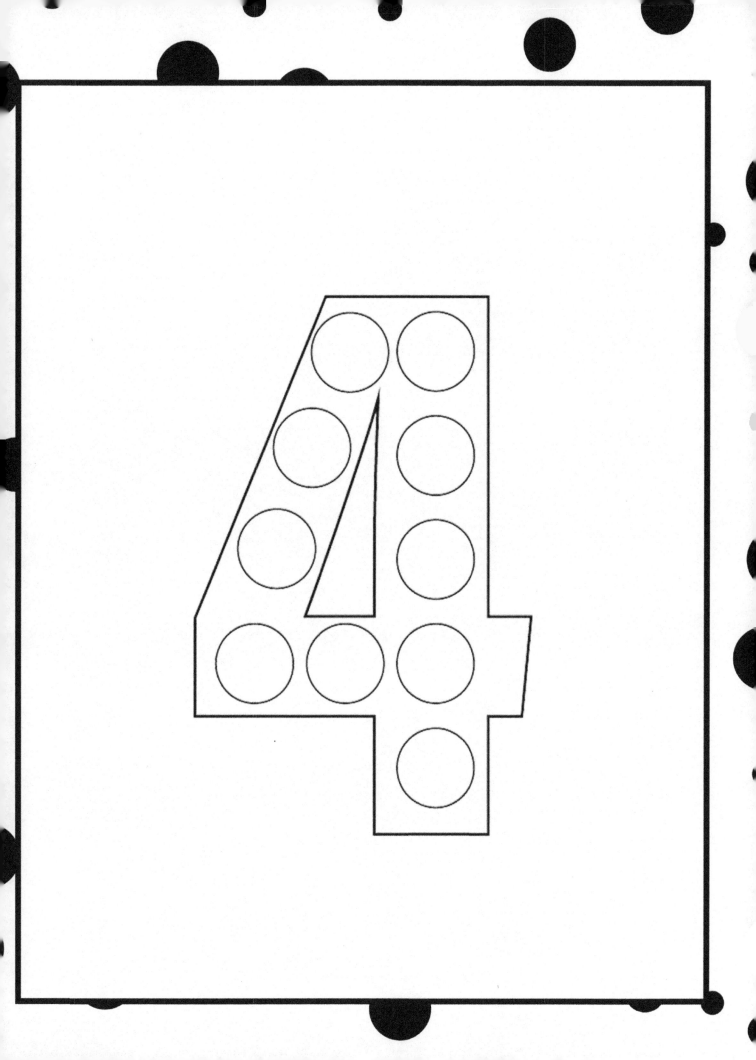

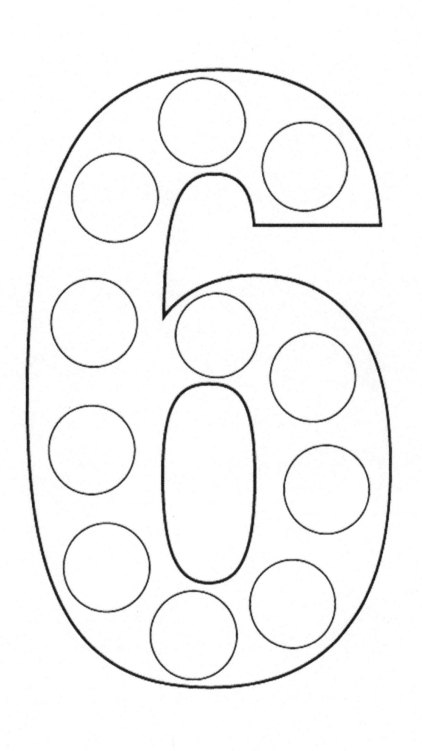

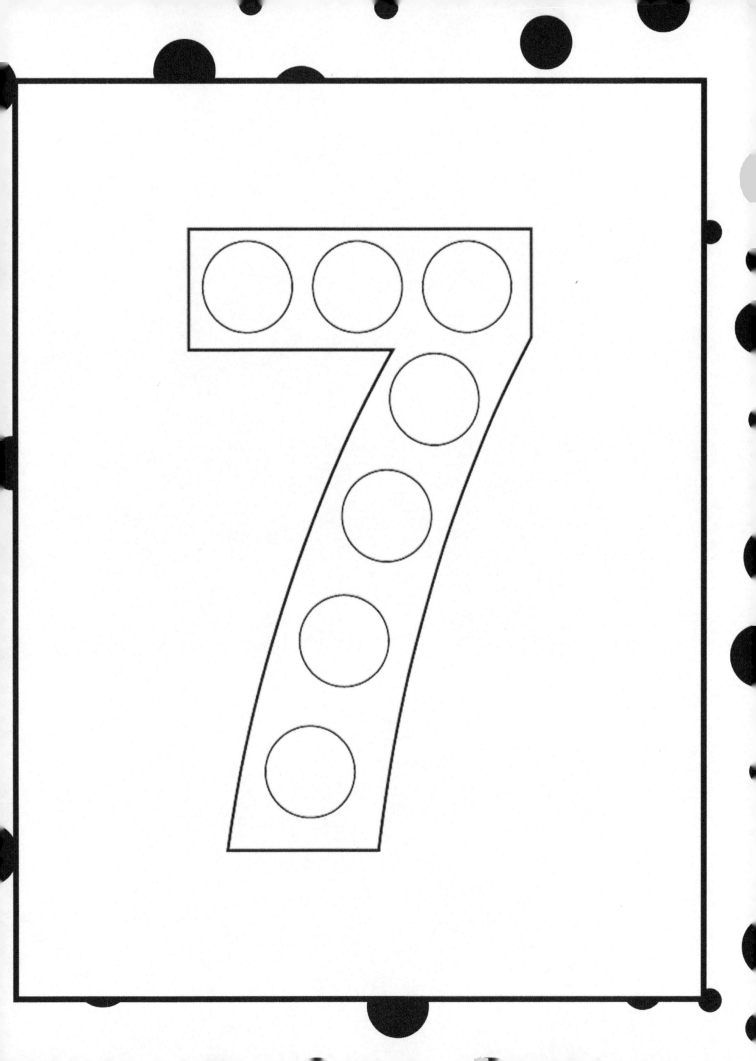

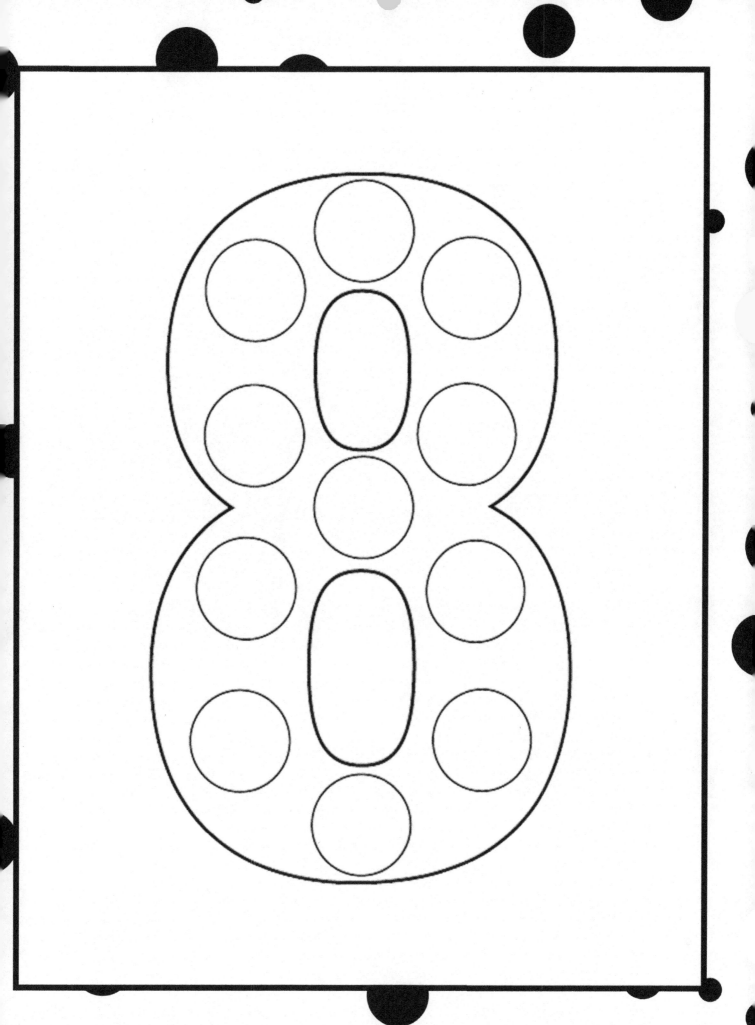

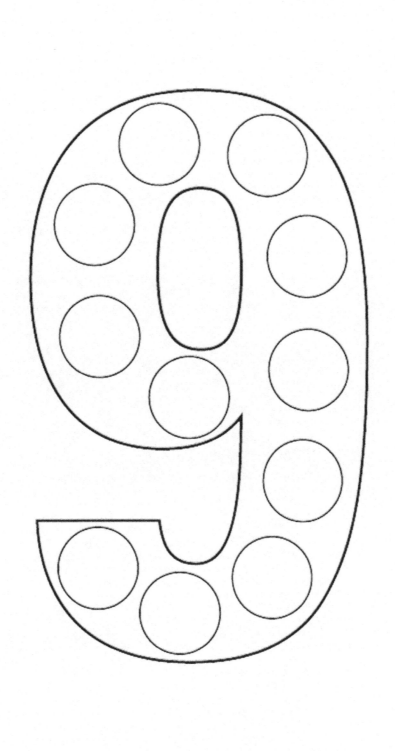

CHAPTER 3
ANIMALS

CHAPTER 4
SHAPES

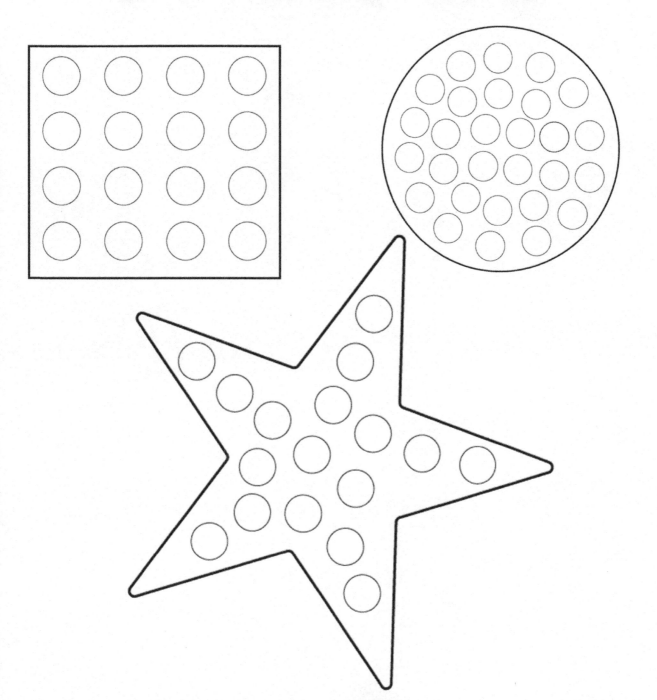

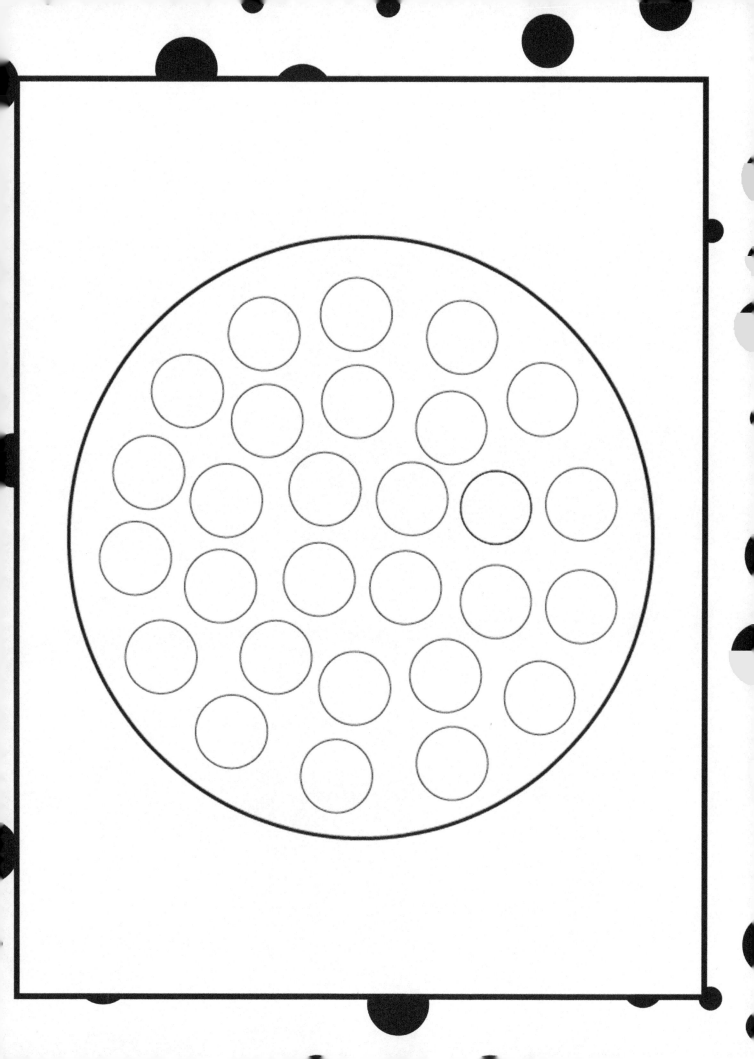

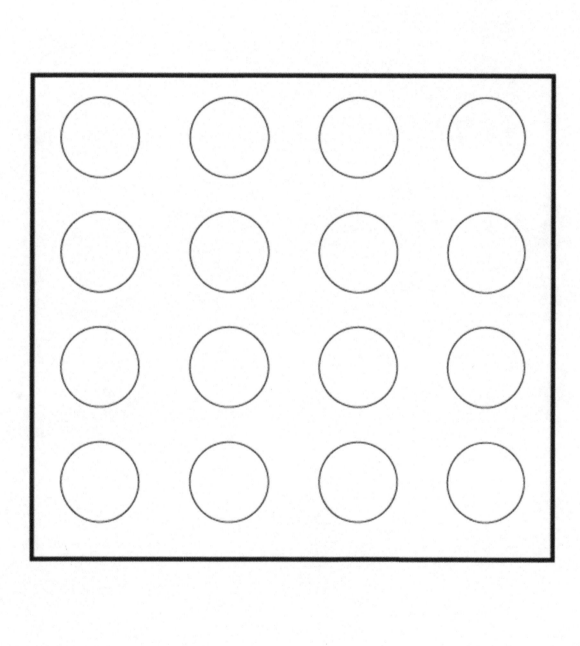

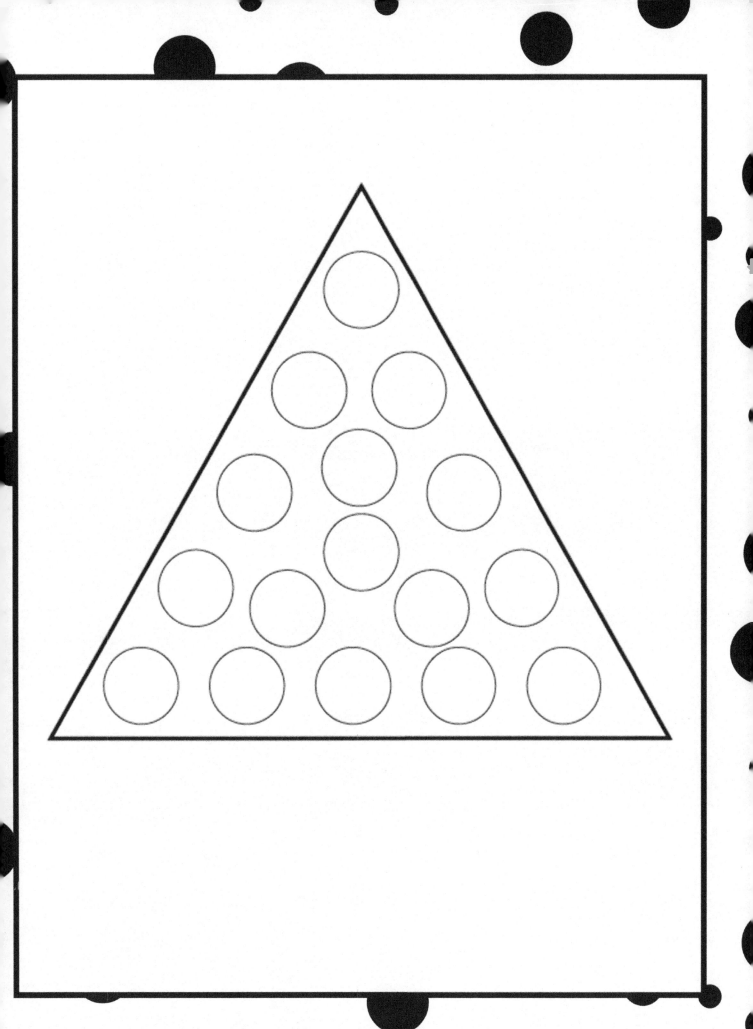

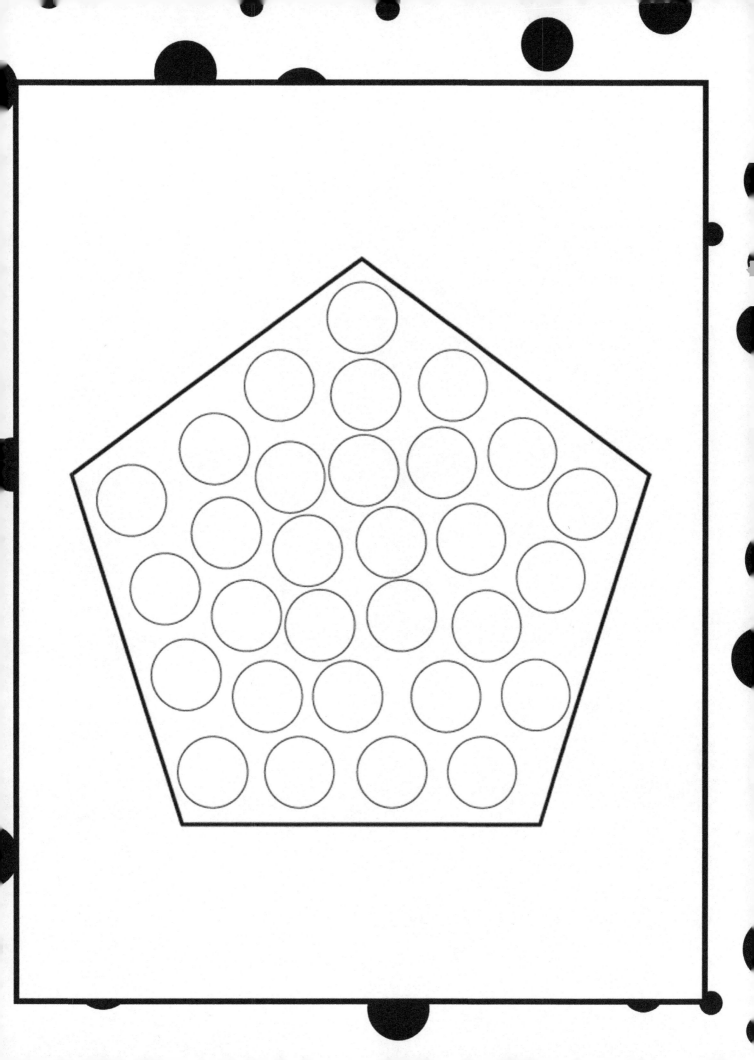

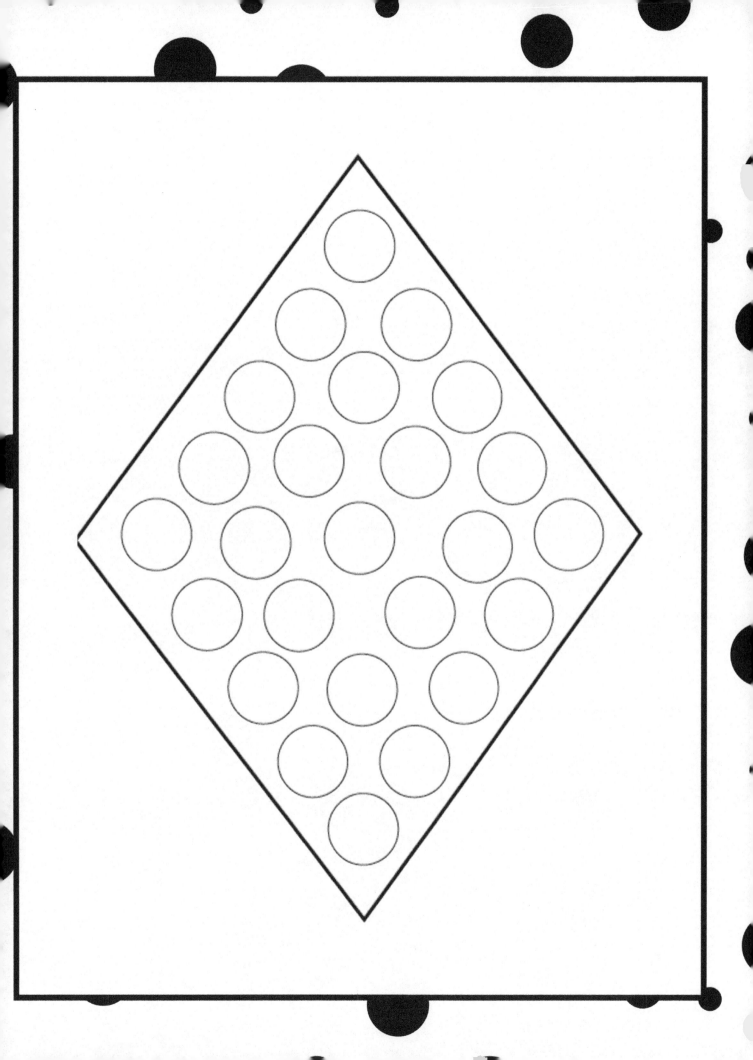

CHAPTER 5
VEHICLES

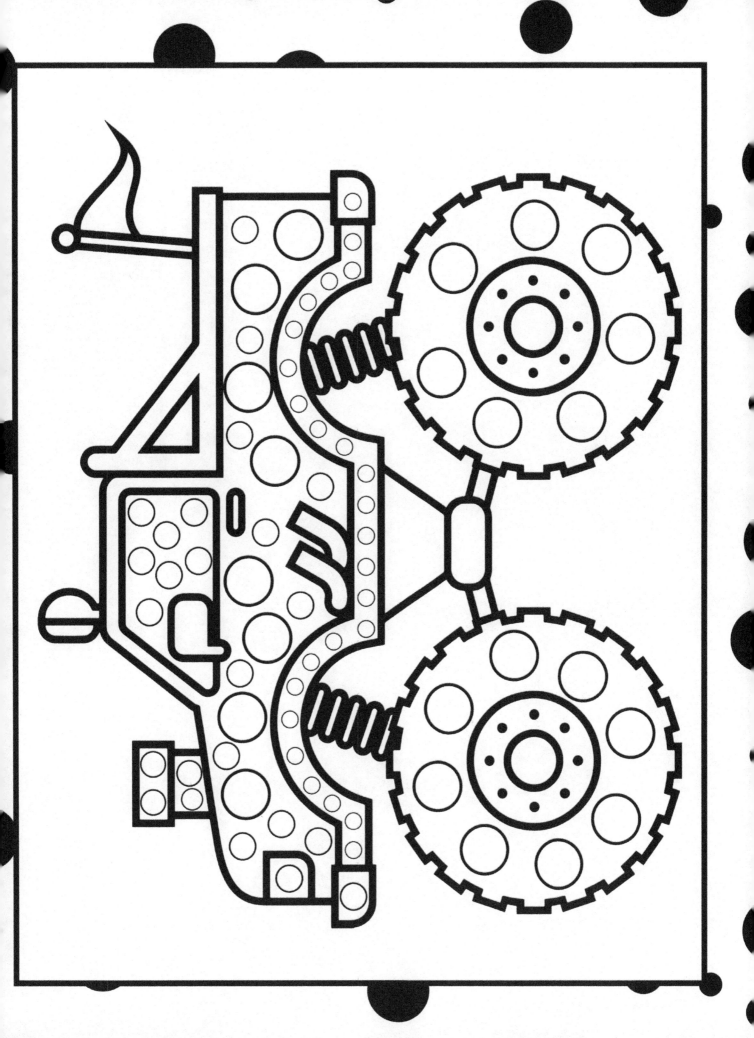

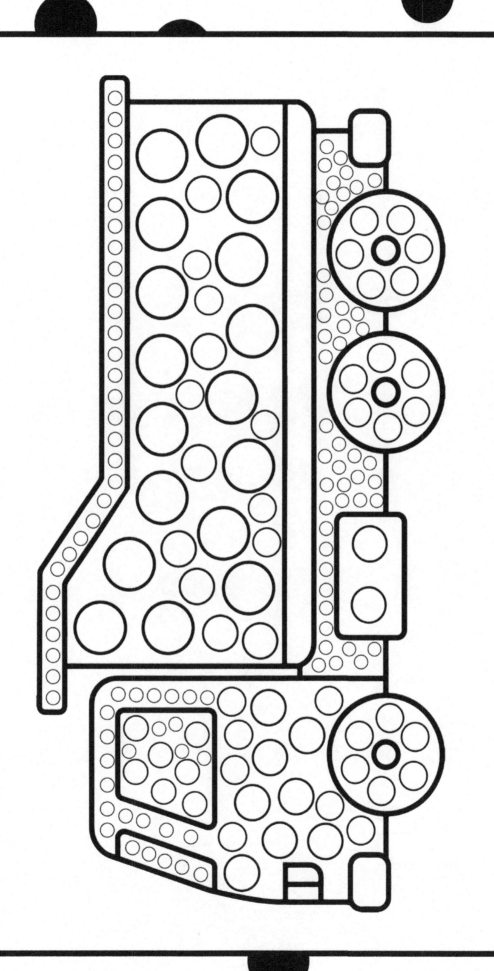

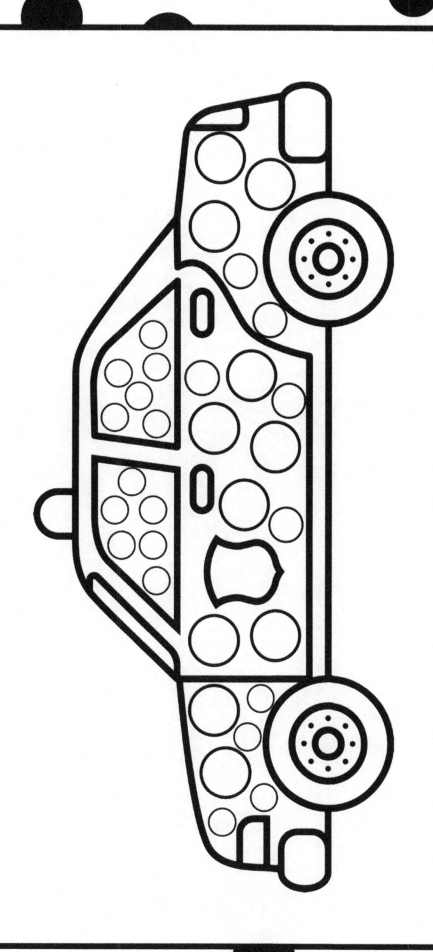

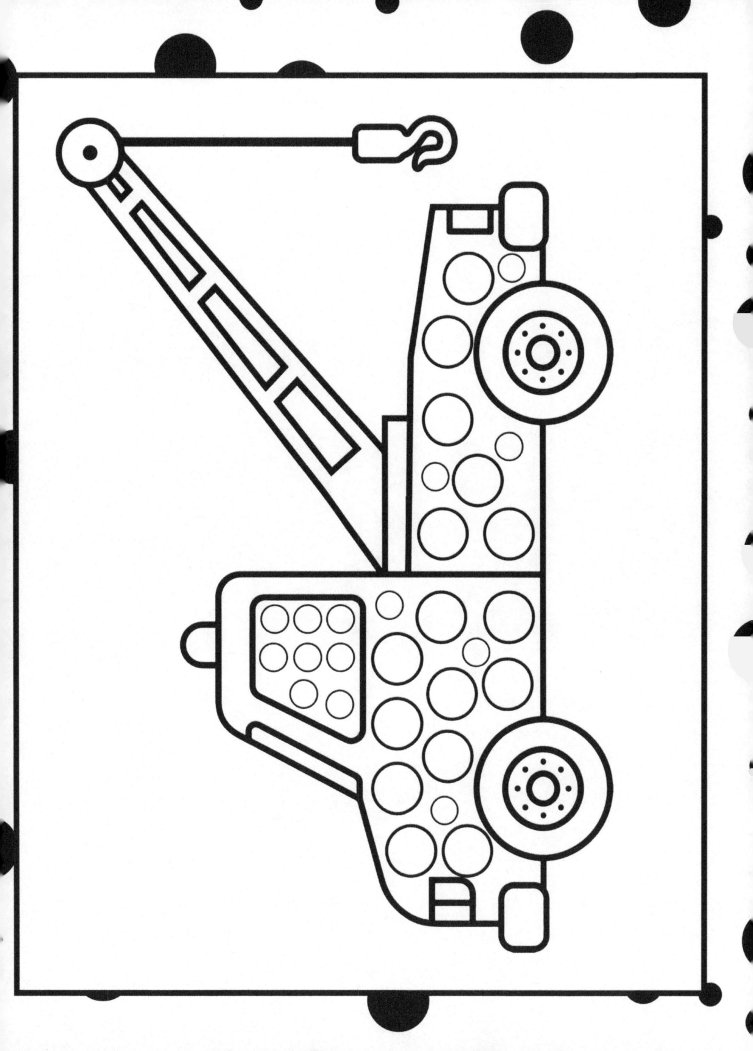

Made in the USA
Las Vegas, NV
24 November 2024

12523438R00063